Emma Kate

To Dr. Seuss and Horton

PATRICIA LEE GAUCH, EDITOR

Copyright © 2005 by Babushka Inc.
PHILOMEL BOOKS   A division of Penguin Young Readers Group
Published by The Penguin Group
Penguin Group (USA) Inc., 375 Hudson Street, New York, NY 10014, U.S.A.
Penguin Group (Canada), 10 Alcorn Avenue, Toronto, Ontario, Canada M4V 3B2 (a division of
Pearson Penguin Canada Inc.)
Penguin Books Ltd, 80 Strand, London WC2R 0RL, England.
Penguin Ireland, 25 St. Stephen's Green, Dublin 2, Ireland (a division of Penguin Books Ltd.)
Penguin Group (Australia), 250 Camberwell Road, Camberwell, Victoria 3124, Australia
(a division of Pearson Australia Group Pty Ltd).
Penguin Books India Pvt Ltd, 11 Community Centre, Panchsheel Park,
New Delhi - 110 017, India.
Penguin Group (NZ), Cnr Airborne and Rosedale Roads, Albany, Auckland 1310,
New Zealand (a division of Pearson New Zealand Ltd).
Penguin Books (South Africa) (Pty) Ltd, 24 Sturdee Avenue, Rosebank,
Johannesburg 2196, South Africa.
Penguin Books Ltd, Registered Offices: 80 Strand, London WC2R 0RL, England.

Published simultaneously in Canada.   Manufactured in China by South China Printing Co. Ltd.

Design by Semadar Megged.   The text was set in Optima.   The art was done in pencils and markers.

Library of Congress Cataloging-in-Publication Data
Polacco, Patricia.   Emma Kate / Patricia Polacco.   p. cm.
Summary: Emma Kate and her best friend share many activities, such as homework and soccer
practice, and even have their tonsils out at the same time!   [1. Best friends—Fiction.
2. Friendship—Fiction. 3. Elephants—Fiction. 4. Imagination—Fiction.]
I. Title.   PZ7.P75186Em 2005   [E]—dc22   2004024507
ISBN 0-399-24452-2
10 9 8 7 6 5 4

Emma Kate

Patricia Polacco

Philomel Books

Emma Kate is my best friend.

We do just about everything together!

We walk to school together every morning.

She sits next to me in class.

We play together at recess.

We sit together in the café-gym-a-torium at lunch.

When we get home from school,
we ride our bikes together.

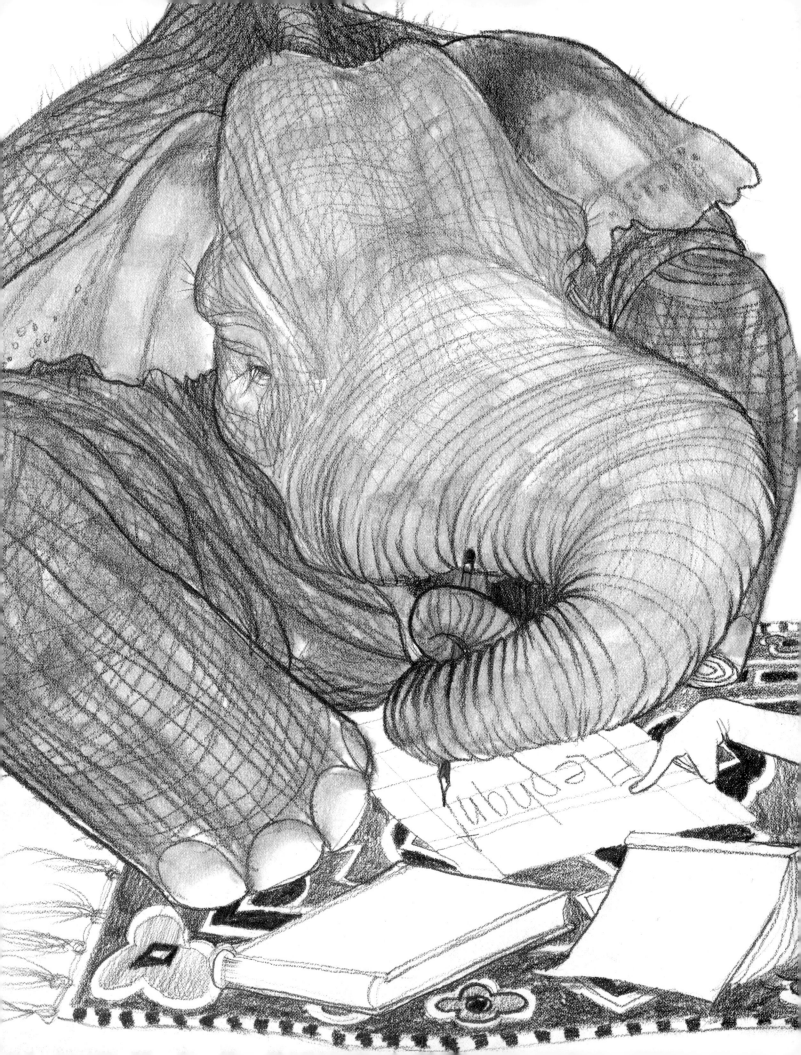

We do our homework together, too!
Sometimes, even on a school night, she stays over.

She loves my pet mouse Gwendolyn.

On weekends, Momma drives us to soccer practice.

We take long walks and watch the clouds in the sky.
Most of all we love to read together.

One day Emma Kate got a real sore throat . . .
—and so did I!
When we went to see the doctor, the doctor said that we would have to have our tonsils out.

So we went to the hospital and got our tonsils out . . .
—then we both ate gallons of pink ice cream!

Emma Kate is my best friend.

We take our baths together.
Then we climb into bed.

Sometimes, when nighttime comes and I'm in my bed, I tell Momma and Daddy all about Emma Kate and the things we do together.

They just smile and say, "You and your Emma Kate. You have such an imagination. Good night, sweetpea. Sweet dreams."

Then they both give me a big kiss and tuck me in.

And I dream of Emma Kate.